FRIENDS OF ACPL

Reading Aloud to Your Child

Research shows that reading books aloud is the single most valuable support parents can provide in helping children learn to read.

- Be a ham! The more enthusiasm you display, the more your child will enjoy the book.
- Run your finger underneath the words as you read to signal that the print carries the story.
- Leave time for examining the illustrations more closely; encourage your child to find things in the pictures.
- Invite your youngster to join in whenever there's a repeated phrase in the text.
- Link up events in the book with similar events in your child's life.
- If your child asks a question, stop and answer it. The book can be a means to learning more about your child's thoughts.

Listening to Your Child Read Aloud

The support of your attention and praise is absolutely crucial to your child's continuing efforts to learn to read.

- If your child is learning to read and asks for a word, give it immediately so that the meaning of the story is not interrupted. DO NOT ask your child to sound out the word.
- On the other hand, if your child initiates the act of sounding out, don't intervene.
- If your child is reading along and makes what is called a miscue, listen for the sense of the miscue. If the word "road" is substituted for the word "street," for instance, no meaning is lost. Don't stop the reading for a correction.
- If the miscue makes no sense (for example, "horse" for "house"), ask your child to reread the sentence because you're not sure you understand what's just been read.
- Above all else, enjoy your child's growing command of print and make sure you give lots of praise. *You are your child's first teacher — and the most important one. Praise from you is critical for further risk-taking and learning.*

— Priscilla Lynch
Ph.D., New York University
Educational Consultant

For Natalya
— N.G.

For my sister, Marguerita
and in memory of our mother, Viola
— G.F.

Text copyright © 1997 by Nikki Grimes.
Illustrations copyright © 1997 by George Ford.
All rights reserved. Published by Scholastic Inc.
HELLO READER!, CARTWHEEL BOOKS, and the
CARTWHEEL BOOKS logo are registered trademarks of Scholastic Inc.

Library of Congress Cataloging-in-Publication Data
Grimes, Nikki.
  Wild, wild hair / by Nikki Grimes ; illustrated by George Ford.
    p.   cm. — (Hello reader! Level 3)
  Summary: In this rhyming story, an African-American girl hides when it's time to comb and braid her hair.
  ISBN 0-590-26590-3
  [1. Hair—Care and hygiene—Fiction.   2. Afro-Americans—Fiction.   3. Stories in rhyme.]
I. Ford, George Cephas, ill.   II. Title.   III. Series.
PZ8.3.G8875Wi   1997   95-21898
[E]—dc20   CIP
                                                                          AC

12 11 10 9 8 7 6 5 4 3 2 1   7 8 9/9 0 1 2/0

Printed in the U.S.A.   23

First Scholastic printing, January 1997

Wild, Wild Hair

by Nikki Grimes
Illustrated by George Ford

Hello Reader! — Level 3

SCHOLASTIC INC. Cartwheel B·O·O·K·S·®

New York   Toronto   London   Auckland   Sydney

But every Monday morning,
Tisa stayed in bed.
She hung onto her pillow.
She dove under the spread.

School was not the problem.
She liked going there.
But Monday was the day
Mommy braided Tisa's hair.

"My hair's a mess," she'd say.
"So what? I'm just a kid."
Tisa said that every week,
and every week she hid.

Her daddy looked for her.
She hid behind a door.
"Come out, Tisa," he would say.
"What are you hiding for?"

Her brother checked the den,
looked up and down the hall.
He walked right by her twice,
pressed flat against the wall.

As always, Tisa's mother
found her behind the stair.
"Let's go," Mommy said.
"It's time to do your hair."

So Tisa balled her fists
and curled up all ten toes.
She closed her eyes.
She made a face.
She said, "Okay. Here goes!"

"Ouch!" she cried before the comb
had touched her head.
Tisa fussed and grumbled,
"I wish I were in bed!"

Her hair was full of knots.
Her mom raked through each one.
Tisa stuck her lip way out
and said, "This is no fun."

"Just cut your hair like mine,"
her brother, Steve, would tease.
"I can brush mine once or twice
and I'm all set to leave."

By now Tisa was sure
to jump out of her skin.
Her mother sighed and said,
"All right. I can begin."

At last, Tisa sat still
as Mommy told her to.
Soon twenty braids were done.
Her mother's fingers flew.

Now Tisa eyed herself.
She couldn't turn away.
Steve rolled his eyes and said,
"The bus won't wait all day!"

Tisa grabbed her coat
and gave her mom a hug.
She even smiled when brother Steve
gave one thick braid a tug.